Twisted: A Cinderella Story

Michelle Robinson

Published by Adorn Creations, 2023.

TWISTED: A CINDERELLA STORY

First edition. April 4, 2023.

ISBN: 979-8223630197

Written by Michelle Robinson.

Table of Contents

1 RAYA ST. THOMAS 1

2 THE SUMMON 7

3 THE QUEEN 17

4 THE FIRST CONTEST 22

5 THE APOLOGY 26

6 Unexpected RETURNS 31

7 Where it all began 35

8 disqualified 39

9 I'm Leaving 43

10 I object 48

The End 61

ABOUT THE AUTHOR 62

1 RAYA ST. THOMAS

"I'm so glad this school year is almost over. It should be a crime to have to wear this shit every day!" Tessa, my best friend, said as Jay and I laughed.

"Well, don't forget tomorrow is freestyle Friday, so we can wear whatever we want." Jay said.

"Fuck a freestyle Friday. I want to wear what I want when I want. I mean really who has to wear uniforms every damn day." Tessa said as I giggled and Jay began to roll her eyes sarcastically.

"And what exactly are you rolling your eyes at?" Tessa asked Jay.

"I'm rolling them at you. The only person complaining," Jay said as her and Tessa began arguing.

As you can see, Jay and Tessa have a love-hate relationship. They have two completely different personalities. Sometimes it's a good thing. Otherwise, well, we all see what's happening now. Tessa has the heart of a lion. Jay is the bookworm. But, then there's me, Raya St. Thomas. I'm both of these girls in one. The main goal I have for myself is to give my mother everything she deserves. I watched her struggle to raise me and I want nothing more than to give her the world and make her happy! Anyways, I needed to put an end to this arguing. I swear they're annoying sometimes.

"Okay, damn. Will the two of you make up already? You argue more than a married couple," I said as they both turned to look at me.

"Well, I guess we'll get married since we're friends for life," Tessa replied as Jay giggled and I rolled my eyes.

"Anyways, I'm out of here. I still have to stop to the market and pick up some fruits before I get home," I informed them and they nodded. I then closed my locker and headed to catch the trolley to the market.

CURRENTLY AT THE PALACE

"There's no way in hell I'm doing that," Prince Corey yelled frustrated.

"Son, this isn't a choice. This has always been the rules," King Louis replied.

"I'm a grown ass man. Can't no one tell me who to marry. I'll pick her myself!" Prince Corey yelled back.

"18 dear. Your only 18 and if you consider yourself a grown man this is even more reason on why you need to marry. I really wish there was another way but this has been the rule for generations," Queen Nia said.

"And there's no other way around this?" Prince Corey asked.

"Well, you could have an audition or ball of some sort." King Louis informed the prince.

"So basically, meeting someone I don't know and train her to be queen. Great. Just fuck my love life." Prince Corey said sarcastically.

"Son, at this point in time I don't give a fuck what you do. I'm ready to step down and travel around the world with your mom. You have 48 hours to make a decision. If not, I will make one for you. Let's go honey." King Louis said as he grabbed the queens' hands and they left Prince Corey to his thoughts.

"And dye your damn hair while you're at it!" Prince Corey yelled back towards the king as he then began to crack up in laughter.

FARMERS MARKET(RAYA)

"Fresh fruit, fresh vegetables. I want to be gone in an hour. At least you can do is spend a dollar!" Joe yelled out.

"What a way to bring the customers in Joe." I said as he then turned to me.

"Raya, it's been a slow week. I have to get this stuff out." Joe told me.

"Well, if it helps any, I'm here for the usual and throw in a couple extra apples will ya." I told Joe.

"You got it," Joe said as he then turned to start bagging up my things. Moments later I felt a hand grab me and moved me to the side and I turned around.

"Hey!" I yelled out in anger.

"Move it lady, the prince is coming through. " The bodyguard said.

"Excuse me, I don't give a damn who he is. He'll wait his turn in line like everyone else." I yelled at the bodyguard.

"Ma'am I'll have you thrown in jail for disobeying an order." The bodyguard said as the prince then approached.

"What's going on here?" He asked.

"Listen buddy, I don't give a damn who you are. I was here first and you will wait just like everyone else." I yelled at the prince as he then turned to his bodyguard.

"I got it from here." He said as the bodyguard then began to walk away. He had me pissed.

"And go get your hair cut while you wait. You look ridiculous!" I yelled at the bodyguard as he walked away and the prince began to laugh as I rolled my eyes.

PRINCE COREY

After that conversation with my parents, I just had to get out of the palace. I decided to go to the Farmers Market to get some fruit from Joe. Everyone knows Joe has the best fruit. As I looked out the window, I see this beautiful girl pointing her fingers as if she was chewing out my bodyguard. I decided to get out the car to see what was going on. Once I walked over not only did, she chew me out but she insulted my bodyguard after I told him I got it from here. I couldn't help but laugh. Who was she?

"So, you come here often?" I asked her.

"Every week." She replied to me with her back turned.

"So that means you live around here then." I said hoping she turn back around so I could see her face and it was that moment she did.

"I'm sure you see the uniform, so yeah. Not everyone can be born in royalty. " She said as she then turned her back towards me again. I couldn't understand it. Woman would die to have a conversation with me or faint just to have me in their presence. She's the only girl I know who knows I'm the prince and not acknowledge me. I'm even more intrigued.

"So do you have a name?" I asked her. I need more information on her. She's a mystery.

"Are we playing 21 questions or something?" She snapped back.

"I mean you haven't asked me any questions so technically no." I responded to her.

"I honestly don't care to know anything about you." She said as she looked me straight in my eyes with her arms crossed. Damn she was beautiful as I looked at the features on her face.

"What do you mean? You know I'm the prince, right?" I asked.

"Yeah, I know who you are. Doesn't mean I want to know you any further." She said as she continued to stare me in my eyes as if she wanted me to see that she meant it.

"Okay Raya, I'm ready for you. This is a bit much so I'll help you take this stuff to the car." Joe said and I can't front. I was saved by the bell.

"Thanks Joe," She said to him with a smile. She then turned to face me.

"Your highness." She said as she then walked away. Raya huh? That's a start. At least now I know her name. Joe then returned.

"What can I do for you today your highness?" Joe asked as I zoned away in my thoughts. I couldn't get her out of my mind and she's only been gone a split second. I then thought of an idea and needed to get back to the castle immediately.

"Joe bag everything up that you have left out here. I'm going to send people from the Palace to come pick it up. Charge it to the palace account please." I told him.

"You got it. " Joe said as I then went to the car and rode back to the palace. I needed to talk to my parents. As I arrived back to the palace, I found my parents in the ballroom.

"Son," King Louis said.

"I want to have an audition. But now just any audition. I want to summon a certain number of girls and choose between them to whichever one I see best fit for queen." I told them.

"And what are you planning to do with them?" my mom asked.

"I will hold contests. Testing skill, knowledge letting them win dates with me to get to know each one of them better." I said as my father then rubbed his chin for a moment.

"Honey?" my mom said as she looked at my father.

"I guess that could work. But that didn't take long. The way you ran in here something obviously had to change your mind." He said curiously. I honestly felt like he didn't need to know. You would think he would have just been glad I got on board.

"Because your right. Someone has to take over and who else is left besides me since Sara and Justin. But father..." I began to say before he cut me off.

"I'm not in the mood to talk about your brother and sister. How long do you expect these auditions to go on?" He asked and I began to get annoyed. I get he's upset with my siblings but I'm the baby and being held accountable for the highest. This shit sucks. Sometimes I wish I could see them again. Just talk to them again. I began to sigh.

"For as long as I need it to so I can make sure I get to know everyone and make the best decision by who I like the most." I said and surprisingly he agreed.

"Fine, inform the workers to let them get rooms ready for these girls." I nodded as I then left out the ballroom. I informed the workers then looked around the palace to find B, my bodyguard. As crazy as my mind is going. I needed all the information I needed on Raya and B was going to find that for me.

2 THE SUMMON

THE NEXT DAY

"And that students is how you put a condom on a banana," Mr. Gibson said as the entire class began to laugh.

"Why do I have to get the childish students this semester." He said as he placed his hand in his head.

"I'd love to out a condom on his banana." Tessa whispered to me as I began to giggle.

"I mean no offense Mr. Gibson but I think everyone here knows how to put a condom on. Unless your name is Tessa of course." Jessica said as Tessa rolled her eyes. Jessica is head captain of the cheerleading team. She thinks she the HBIC when she's not. She's just a spoil little brat who thinks she can do whatever because her family lives good.

"OH? Because that's not what your brother said when I put it on with my..." Tessa began to say before Mr. Gibson interrupted her.

"Okay! Can everyone please just turn to Chapter 5 please?" Mr. Gibson asked.

"Mr. Gibson. What's chapter 5 on?" Jay asked curiously.

"Female orgasms." He said as everyone busted into laughter and all he could do was shake his head. He then began to teach until class was over.

AFTER CLASS

"I swear I come to school just to go to sex education. Jessica makes me want to slap the hell out her. It's not my fault she couldn't keep her legs closed and Kenny came running into my arms." Tessa said to Jay and I. Kenny was Jessica's boyfriend for three years until she cheated on him. He is the captain of the football team. Once he found out he found comfort in Tessa and they slept together. Jessica hated us ever since.

"And besides, Kenny could take some lessons from Mr. Gibson. He was weak in bed." Tessa said and we laughed.

"Girl, you are obsessed with Mr. Gibson." I told her.

"Don't you see how fine he is? I got a couple tricks or two for his ass." Tessa said and Jay and I laughed again.

"So, I met our beloved prince yesterday. " I told them and their mouths dropped.

"Um, that is not a secret you keep overnight." Jay said.

"Right. Did you sleep with him?" Tessa asked and we laughed at her.

"Is that all you ever think about? And no, I did not sleep with him. Unlike the two of you I was very annoyed with his presence and I wanted to kick his bodyguard's ass." I said as Tessa then turn to Jay to whisper in her ear and they began a secretive conversation.

"What the hell are the two of you going on about?" I asked.

"Oh, Nothing. Just how we should slap the hell out you for being so stupid!" Tessa yelled as Jay began to crack up.

"How the hell could you not jump in the arms of the finest man in this country?" Tessa asked.

"Yeah Raya, what's up with that?" Jay asked.

"Maybe I don't find him attractive like you two idiots." I replied to them.

"Are you out of your damn mine?" Jay asked as Tessa turned to face her.

"She totally is. Is it crack? I think she's smoking crack." Tessa said as Jay busted out in laughter.

"I hate both of you!" I said as I then began to walk away from them to head to the restroom.

"Wait, don't go yet. You forgot to tell us what his penis look like." Tessa yelled out and Jay laughed again. I swear they would be the death of me.

As I was ready to flush, I heard Jessica walking in the bathroom talking loudly as if she was the only one in here.

"So, you know my mom has friends higher up. And she was told that the prince is having auditions for queen because the king is ready to step down." Jessica told Sherry her best friend. How the hell can you force someone to be queen? I thought to myself as I rolled my eyes.

"That's exciting. So, are you going to audition?" Sherry asked.

"Of course. My invitation was personal." Jessica said.

"I hope I get a letter." Sherry said. These girls were pathetic. I decide to flush so they can know they were not alone. I then walked out the stall to the sink and I could feel them staring.

"We have a little eavesdropper I see." Sherry said.

"Well, if it isn't miss priss." Jessica said as I then turned around to shake the water, I had on my hands towards them.

"First off dumb and dumber, no one has to eavesdrop. Your voices so deep the whole school can hear you." I said as I crossed my arms waiting for a comeback.

"Excuse me?" Jessica said.

"Your heard me right and get your lashes fix will ya. You look like Bob the builder." I said as I then cracked up and she frowned with her arms crossed.

"But hey, who am I to judge?" I said as I walked out of the bathroom laughing.

AT THE PALACE

"Move your asses! We need to get this place in order! Mrs. Daisy moves faster than this shit" I yelled. I then see B come in.

"What's up B? You look like shit today" I said and he laughed.

"Anyways I got what you asked for. I got as much information on the girl as I could." He said and in this moment nothing else matter. I just want to know who *she* is.

"Her name is Raya St. Thomas. 17 years old. She has an upcoming birthday. She's a Senior this year and an only child. Her father died while her mother was pregnant with her. Straight A student. She's spontaneous, level-headed, determined and has a mind of her own. She's a perfect candidate for queen sir." B informed me and I was even more intrigued.

" Very very interesting. Make sure she is summoned to the palace personally. And I don't want anything or anyone standing in her way before she gets here and even after." I told B.

"Yes, sir I'll go get her now." He said and I nodded. I just had to know why the hell she isn't impressed with me.

MRS. ST. THOMAS

The door rang. I didn't understand who would be knocking when we weren't expecting anyone. I looked through the peep hold to see this man standing outside my door. Who the hell is he? I then opened the door.

"Can I help you?" I asked.

"Mrs. St. Thomas. I'm B and I work for the palace." He said and I was even more confused.

"The palace? I'm surprised to one of you down here in such a poor town. What can I do for you?" I asked curiously.

"I'm here for your daughter." The man replied.

"My daughter? What the hell has my daughter done?" I asked frustrated.

"She has been summoned to the palace to audition for queen." He said as I paused for a moment before I began to chuckle.

"Queen? How can you force someone to be queen? But I'm sorry, my daughter is only 17 years old and I do not want that type of responsibility on her." I said to him.

"This is not a request this is an order from the king and queen. Failure to comply will result in jail time. You have exactly one hour to make your decision. " The man said before he walked out the door and my mouth dropped as I was shocked. This was really happening. This was some bullshit. This was never something I wanted to put my 17-year-old daughter through.

I began to scream in anger. I have to talk to her. If it's something she wants to do then so be it. If not then I have no problem going to jail for my daughter. I hate my life right now. I sighed. As I turned around Raya was right there.

"Wow mom, do I really cause so much trouble in your life?" She asked and a part of my heart broke.

"Oh no sweetie you could never. You are the best part of my life." I told her and she looked at me confused.

"It was a joke mom. Don't get all mushy on me." She said as she giggled but I meant every word.

"What's going on with you? Why aren't you laughing?" She asked and I sighed.

"Sit down sweetie, we need to talk." I told her as she nodded and we both sat down on the living room couch.

PRINCE COREY

The time has finally arrived. Was I ready to be king? I was only 18 years old. Will the people of this country respect me? Will she hate me for forcing her to get to know me? I began to breathe deeply as I continued my thoughts. I have to get my shit together.

"I'm back for a moment prince." B said as I then turned around to him.

"She'll be here no worries. I just wanted to update you personally." B said. "I'm going back to pick her up now I just wanted to let you know." He continued to say.

"Good." I said as he walked off and I sighed. Guess I'll gather my parents so we can make our introductions to these girls.

RAYA

"Are they out of their damn minds? How can they force someone to audition for queen? They are not going to force my mother to do anything!" I yelled.

"Raya I'll never make you do anything you don't want to do. I know this is not what you want and I personally don't want that type of responsibility on you at this age." Mom said.

"Mom, I know you love me and I know you would do anything for me. But I can't have you go to jail. I wouldn't survive without you. I mean it's just an audition right. It's not like I'm going to get chosen anyways. My acting skills are horrible. " I said as my mom chuckled.

"Are you sure about this sweetie?" She asked.

"Yes, I refuse for you to be chained and handcuffed. But I am confused about something. " I informed her.

"And what's that?" She asked.

"I heard a girl in the bathroom saying selected girls were supposed to get a summoned letter. Why would they come here?" I asked.

"Maybe they ran out of paper." She said as we both paused for a moment before busting out in laughter.

"They ran out of paper mom really?"

"I didn't know what else to say." She said as we chuckled again and the doorbell rang.

"I guess I'll get ready now. I love you mom." I said and she brought me in for a tight hug.

"I love you too and you'll always be my baby no matter what." She said as she then let me go and I headed to my room to pack some belongings.

MRS. ST. THOMAS

As the doorbell rang, I waited a few moments to give Raya time to get some of her things. When I looked through the peep hole it was that man again. I rolled my eyes before opening the door.

"Have you made your decision?" He asked.

"My daughter will be down in a second you nugget head bastard." I told him with my arms crossed annoyed.

"Is all that even necessary?" He asked and before I could respond I heard Raya's voice.

"I should have known when my mother mentioned jail talk you were the one behind it. Maybe if I asked if it was a man with the reallyyy bad hairline I would have known who came here." Raya said.

"His hairline really is bad." I said as Raya and I cracked up.

"I mean I am standing right here. Can we just get going place?" the man said as he placed his head in his hand.

"Ok fine. What is your name again?" Raya asked.

"You can just call me B" He said.

"OMG is it '**B**' cause your ugly?" Raya asked with so much excitement all we could do was crack up. If it was anything my daughter and I had in common, it was our sense of humor.

"Damn women, I'll be in the car," B said as he walked out and Raya turned to me.

"I love you mom," She said as she hugged me.

"I love you too sweetie," I said I eventually let her go as she headed to the car and left.

CURRENTLY AT THE PALACE

"I'm sorry Sherry. I love you, but the crown is mine," Jessica said as Sherry rolled her eyes sarcastically.

"Sure, whatever you say," Sherry replied.

"I can't believe I got chosen to audition for queen. I never get chosen for anything!" Rose said with excitement out loud as the girl next to her turns to look at her.

"Yeah, that's too bad, because I'm going to sweep the rug with all of you peasants," Sydney said to Rose while laughing, as Rose crossed her arms with angry face annoyed.

"I'm such a loser. Why am I even here? I don't want to be queen. Can I just go home now?" Bella said to herself as she stayed away from everyone.

"To bad Raya didn't get pick. I would have loved to kick both of you bitches asses fair and square," Tessa said as Jay rolled her eyes.

"Says the first person here who's going to get cut," Jay said as she laughed and Tessa crossed her arms with anger.

A few moments later, the prince, king and queen arrive in the entry hall.

"Good evening, ladies, I'm Prince Corey as you all know. This is my mother Queen Nia and my father King Louis. As you all know the reason," He began to say as the front door slammed.

"You're late." Prince Corey yelled frustrated.

"I'm sorry honey, I was forced to be here, right?" Raya said as Prince Corey looked at her in shock.

PRINCE COREY

I could sense everyone looking at me to see what my response was going to be. Even though she's the only one I wanted here, I cannot let that show at least not right now.

"Don't feel special. Every other lady here today has been forced to be here. Perhaps someone should provide you the definition of summoned," I said to her harshly.

"Well unlike you, I don't have the authority to tell the man speed up the "carriage", She replied sarcastically. What is it about this girl? She won't let up. I'm trying to be as nice as I can before my mother and father get involved.

"Your disrespect right now will not go unanswered. For now, keep your mouth shut and listen to what you clearly interrupted, " I told her as I watched her roll her eyes. I turned to look at my parents who were furious.

"Now as you all know the reason you are here today. If you do not, I'm going to tell you. You ladies have been handpicked specifically for a chance to become not only my bride but as queen. There were 25 candidates and 5 of you were selected by myself while my parents selected one as she is already a princess at our alliance kingdom. Other criteria were based off your age, your grades in school played a part as all of you here are seniors and are at the top of your class. The personality quiz you take at the beginning of the year gives us some insight about who you are as a person. As there are other key factors, it's not relevant right now and I would like to be the first to say congratulations to all of you for making the cut and thank you for being here today." I said as everyone clapped and I looked as Raya as she clapped sarcastically and rolled her eyes. She's definitely going to be a tough one to crack. Next thing you know I see all the ladies bowing as I watched my mother walk up and began to speak.

"Good evening, ladies." She said and I just prayed she didn't kick Raya out before everything started.

3 THE QUEEN

RAYA

I watched as the queen come forward with a frown on her face. She's staring at me like a piece of meat and mostly because of how I treated the prince. Well, if the royal family thinks forcing me to come here is a display of power, I'll show them how stubborn I can be. I will not be forced by anyone. Not even the king.

"I'd like to thank you all for coming here on such notice. It must have been stressful to pack up and come here just like that. Accept my apologies on that part," the queen said, staring at the bags we all had next to us. I looked around and found the biggest bag of all right beside Jessica. Typical. I wondered how much makeup and jewelry she had packed there. Enough to start a salon, I'm sure.

"I don't want to waste you lovely ladies' time so I'll get right to the point." Her face hardened in a frown.

"We will be holding contests to select the bride. Five certain contests. Every girl standing here is already worth ten points. For everyone who succeeds the contests, they get two points. Those who fail lose two points. Those who do the best get an extra point and the best scorer in each contest will get a date with the prince as a reward. The overall best lady will be the prince's bride."

The prince smiled and waved and every girl standing swooned except me. That smug little bastard.

"What happens to the person with the lowest scores at the end of the contests?" I asked. If it was something mild, I would intentionally fail each contest and escape the damned palace. None of this nonsense made enough sense for me to anticipate it.

The queen looked annoyed when she eyed me. "Nothing will happen to them BUT," a small smirk spread on her face, "while you're in the palace, every contest you fail will grant you a punishment so don't even think about failing intentionally. Also, if you disrespect royalty too much, your family outside will bear the consequences so be careful how you behave while in the palace walls."

It was my turn to frown. "So, every time I fail to be a perfect, forced princess, I get punished?" I implied.

"Watch your mouth, girl." The queen expressed angrily.

"Oh, this is me watching it. Imagine when I don't." I snapped back.

The queen was fuming now. I know I'm threading on thin lines but I'm very angry too. I'm being forced to play little princess against my will and still be putting my mother in trouble from here. Royalty was bullshit.

The king cleared his throat, dragging everyone's attention to him. "You must all be tired. The maids will escort you to your rooms and help you unpack. I hope the rest of your stay here will be, well as you children say it, fun." He smiled wildly and the girls all smiled back. The queen and I we're still raging but I went ahead with the girls and the maids while she went to sit beside her husband.

I already hated it here and it hasn't been an hour yet.

PRINCE COREY

I watched Raya leave the hall with a frown. She was a spitfire, ready to take on anyone even if it put her in trouble. It was an admirable attitude but faced against the queen, it could put her in trouble. My mother gripped the hand of her chair in annoyance.

"Mother..." I breathed out sarcastically.

"That girl can NOT become your bride. She's too rude." She demanded.

"I mean, we did call then out without their permission." My father reminded her.

"We are the rulers of this kingdom. The only thing they have to do is obey the little things we ask them to do. How is that difficult?"

I kept quiet. My mother, Queen Nia was a spitfire as well and I wondered day after day how my father managed to make her settle with him despite how much she hated stuffy places and the palace was the epitome of stuffy places. She had changed quite a lot of the royal home after they were crowned.

My father stared at us with a grin. "She looks like fun."

"Louis!" My mother yelled.

"What? That's exactly how you were when we first met at the ball. Well, maybe a little less impolite but more cunning than a female fox. I feel for you right then and there." He held her hands tightly. "And I still love you to this day."

Mother blushed brightly and kissed him. "I love you too. But this child..."

"Well look on the bright side, the first contest is to weed out the best in politeness. If she fails that, she'll be forced to learn etiquette from you. I'm sure you'll enjoy teaching her." My father informed my mother.

My mother smiled, a little devilish one. I felt a small cold on my back. My mother was a scary perfectionist.

RAYA

I looked around the room arranged perfectly. Despite how much I disliked the palace, I had to admit they had good taste in interior decoration. I bounced on my bed and absolutely loved how easily it bounced. It was amazing.

A knock sounded at my door and I turned to it.

"Come in."

Tessa and Jay walked in arguing about something at the same time. I sighed, watching them bucker as they neared my bed and sat on it.

"The queen is all elegant. How can you not like that?" Jay asked.

"The prince looks better," Tessa argued. They both turned to me at the same time like twins. "Who do you prefer in the royal family?"

"The king. He's like aged wine, you know?" He also didn't get on my nerves the way the others did.

Tessa and Jay went quiet for a while before smiling and agreeing. We all burst out laughing and settled into the bed, talking about the contests. Tessa asked me what I thought the first contest would be but a knock came again, drawing our attention. Before we could respond, the door opened and Jessica entered.

"You little sluts managed to sleep your way into this, didn't you?" She barked. She looked angry to be in the contests with us knowing how much better we were than her. Typical insecurity. "I'll make sure you three are dropped in the first week." She marched out and slammed the door behind her.

"...yeah, she's crazy."

"Ever since she and Sherry disbanded over the contest, she's been running mad. I honestly think something deeper is going on there." Jay stated, but I just stared at the door in thought. Was she challenging me? I'll make sure she enjoys every single contest. I had no intention to win but dragging her down with me wouldn't hurt.

4 THE FIRST CONTEST

RAYA

The next day, we lined up the royal garden, waiting for the queen to address us. The girls have all dressed themselves to the brim was I wasn't having any of that. I wore a gray hoodie and my faded jeans with sneakers. If it was offensive to look normal among everyone else with fancy dresses and heels, cuff me.

The queen walked into the garden with a bright smile on her face. I'm sure she enjoys seeing us standing around like hungry peasants asking for her to feed us her precious son. Royalty was getting on my nerves even more than usual.

"Good morning, ladies," she started, crossing her arms behind her. Two maids stood behind her. "I hope you all had a wonderful night. Judging by how beautiful you look this morning; I'll guess I'm right." She looked at me and frowned. "At least some of you."

I rolled my eyes.

"I will announce the first contests so you all can carry on with your day." The Queen informed us.

One of the maids came forward with a basket in her hands. She offered it to each of us to pick a paper from it. "On each piece of paper you've picked, there's a name there. The person on your list is the name of the maids who will help you in this contest." The maids all came out and lined up behind her. "The contest is really simple. Learn palace etiquettes in two days. The maid you picked will assist you in whatever you want while you learn. Any questions?"

I raised my hand. "My paper's blank."

Another hand one went up. It was Sydney. "Me too."

Two other hands went up with the same complaint.

The queen smiled. "I only set 21 maids. The four of you will have to learn on your own so just blame it on your luck. Any complaints?"

The three girls all looked sad but didn't ask anything. I was annoyed again. "It's unfair to us if we don't have anyone to help us."

"It's not like you want to be here. Why are you complaining?"

I was even more annoyed but didn't say anything.

The maids all went to the girls who had picked their names while me, Sydney and the two other girls watched. The queen dismissed the meeting and walked out with the two maids she came with. She didn't want to win. Unfortunately for her, I wanted the exact same thing.

PRINCE COREY

I watched the girls and their maids from my balcony. Raya was the only girl not dressing her best. Her hair was in a messy ponytail and her hoodie had what looked like ketchup stain. I was even more attracted to her carefree attitude. Although I called for the contests, I wanted her to win. She was the best woman I had ever laid my eyes on even though she was still 17. Wait. She's 17. That means her birthday is in a few days.

I remembered B telling me that she was nearly 18 so I had called her in. She was the second youngest along the girls but without a doubt, the most mature. She was more intriguing than the first time we met and I was even more attracted to her.

The maids were teaching the girls to curtsey and stand properly but she stood at the side, slouching intentionally. I knew it was intentional because I knew how well she walked with grace despite not being royal. She was doing it to get on the other girl's nerve and it was working.

A girl I found out was named Jessica had walked up to her and was saying something. Raya was smiling at her and said something that made the girl angry. She raised her hand to hit Raya. I immediately left my spot on the balcony to rush down and stop them.

By the time I got there, the girl was on the floor, crying.

I look at Raya standing there and staring at me with an eyebrow raised.

"What are you doing here?"

I stepped back a bit. She looked angry to see me. "I just came to see if you were fine. I was watching from the balcony when she-"

"What, you're worried about me?" She scoffed and started to walk away." "Maybe you should have been worried before calling me here to play princess with your puppets. Don't talk to me, Corey."

She called me by my name, something only royalty was allowed to do. I watched her leave and head inside, not turning back till the end.

RAYA

It's the next day and time for the contest to start. I watched the girls practice over and over how to curtsey, fake smiles, giggle like annoying Barbies and even learn to eat like royalty. It was sickening to watch them act something they were not just to impress the queen but it's not my place to judge. Tessa and Jay seem to be excited by how much they twirled in their dresses at their spots. We were standing in a line right before the queen's seat, waiting for the contest to begin and we all wore dresses from the royal wardrobe.

In a few minutes, the queen entered and we began. The girls marched up to her and greeted her softly while she asked a question for them to answer. I couldn't hear she asked from where I stood.

"You ready to fail, little peasant?" Jessica said, smiling maliciously. For whatever reason, she stood in front of me in the line.

"I should be asking you that question," I bit back. She had tried to make me fail by putting a red stain on my dress the night before but I knew she would try something so I took a different dress that looked exactly the same right before we came out.

Well, I ripped the bottom of her dress so she would trip and fall when she walked. Two could play that game.

It was her turn to come out and she cat walked elegantly. That is, until she trips on her dress. I snorted when she fell and walked forward to queen. The queen looked angry when she saw me greet perfectly. Today, I would do good to annoy Jessica and her but from here on out, I wasn't gonna be playing royalty anymore.

5 THE APOLOGY

RAYA

It's the next day and I was sitting with Tessa and Jay on my balcony. We just finished eating and we were talking about what happened last night at the contest.

"Jessica looked so embarrassed, I had to cover my mouth to not laugh out loud," Tessa said as she laughed again.

"I didn't cover my mouth. I just burst into laughter," Jay laughed. "I'm sure that took out some of my points cos that laugh was definitely unladylike."

We all laughed. Jessica had been a thorn in our flesh since middle school. After she had tripped, she ran away in embarrassment and the contest continued. The winner of the contents was Sherry and right now, she was on a date with the prince.

"I really wanted to win this one though," Tessa sighed.

Jay leaned back on the chair and sighed too. "Yeah, winning wouldn't be too bad."

"You guys seem really into this," I said.

"Well, we'll be set for life if we managed to bag the next king," Jay said.

"And he looks really good in bed," Tessa giggled.

I rolled my eyes at her and Jay flicked her forehead, causing her cry out in pain and flick her back.

"The next contest should be announced in the afternoon after Sherry gets back," I said.

Tessa checks her phone. "It's about time even. They said it's by 12 and it's 11:57 right now. Should we start going?"

"Yeah, let's go now." Jay stood up and dragged me along. We went to the garden where we met last time and saw the other girls were already waiting. Talk about thirsty and eager. A few minutes later, the queen entered with a blushing Sherry. Sherry joined us in the lineup and the girls all gathered her, asking how the date went. I rolled my eyes at them and turned my attention to the queen. She was smiling at Sherry. It seemed she already chose her. Fine by me.

"Ladies, focus." She clapped once and they all straightened back up. "The next contest will be a simple one. Flower arrangements." A maid came forward with a trolley filled with similar vases, shears, ribbons and everything needed for plucking flowers in a garden. We all picked one and held it. "You all have an hour to arrange the best flowers you can and bring them to me. The best flower arrangement wins this round. Any questions?"

We were silent.

"Good, begin."

The girls started to rush around with the garden equipment and begun to look for flowers in the garden. Tessa and Jay waved at me before leaving, giggling and talk as they start looking for flowers. I picked a pair of scissors and a ribbon and began to walk around.

As expected of a royal garden, the place was lined with amazing, rare and beautiful flowers that I'd seen and I'd never seen. I walked around a bit more, selecting the flowers that catch my eye. I've come to realize that I don't even need to try to lose as the girls all want to win. They'll do excellent jobs to win so all I have to do is have fun. This is the palace. Being here won't happen again.

I filled my vase with different colors of flowers, from white to yellow, to blue and especially purple. I sat on the flowers to trim and prune and arrange the with the ribbons until I was satisfied. A small bell rang out and I realized that an hour had passed in a blink. I loved flowers. It was only natural for me to get lost in then.

We set our vases on the trolley again, waiting for the queen to address us. Instead of the queen inspecting it, the prince walked into the garden, leaving the girls swooning again. I swear, if I rolled my eyes one more time, I'll have them stuck in the back of my head.

He greeted us and began to inspect the flowers, going from one to the other and scrutinizing them. The girls were pulling their hair out of their hair but I couldn't be bothered. I liked my flowers and I didn't care if he did.

After he's done inspecting them, he goes to stand next to his mother. "I've made a decision based on my favorite colors, flowers and arrangement. I choose this vase."

I froze. His hand was on my vase, meaning he chose it. His mother looked at him in shock and so did the girls.

"You must be making a mistake," I said.

"No, these are my favorites."

"That doesn't make any sense."

"I guess we just have similar taste."

The queen looked stumped but so did I. I could feel the glared digging into my skin from where I stood. If the girls had a chance, they'd tear me to bits.

"Well," the queen said, finally collecting herself. "The date will be this evening by 5." She stood up, seemingly angry at the results. "I hope you both have fun together."

No, you don't.

The prince smiled at me, something I didn't appreciate as I stomped off right after the queen did. Damn royals.

PRINCE COREY

I hadn't even realized the vase I had picked was hers until I saw her face. She had picked most of my favorite flowers and the arrangement was beautiful. It seemed we had more in common than I thought. But sitting here with her, with the sunsetting behind her and her curly hair blowing into her face from the ponytail, I realized that I needed to do more to get her to like me.

"You're not saying anything. Did you only choose me so you could stare at me?" She said, munching the cupcake in her hand. It seemed like she had a sweet tooth.

"You're really beautiful."

She rolled her eyes. "You'll need to do better than that, your Highness."

I leaned forward on the chair. I needed to set things straight. "I'd like to apologize."

She froze.

"For bringing you here against your will and making you do this," I said, hoping to lighten her view of me. "I had to choose a way to get a bride, just like all the past kings did. I didn't have a choice."

She frowned. "Why didn't you just hold a ball like the usual?"

"Because I met you." Her frown lessened for a second before coming back on. "I can't just be with any random person. Then, I went out for a breather and I met you. Bold, brave Raya confident enough to stand against a guard. You entranced me."

She didn't say anything and continued to eat her cupcake.

"I'm really sorry for bringing you here like this without your permission but I really wanted to know you," I said and stood up. "But I can't force you to feel the same way so I'll not hold you against your will. If you want to fail intentionally, I won't stop you. I don't want you to be uncomfortable here so I'll leave now. Good night, Raya."

"Wait," she called, pulling my sleeve. She was still frowning but more in distrust than her usual annoyance.

"Yes?"

"I'm not busy for the rest of today," she said. I saw a small blush creep onto her face. "We can hang out and watch the sunset. If you want."

I stared at her in disbelief. Was she real?

"But you can go if you don't want to-"

"I want to!" I said, sitting back and smiling. "Thank you, Raya."

The blush deepened but she looked away and didn't reply. I guess I do have a shot at winning her.

6 Unexpected RETURNS

RAYA

I rolled around on my bed, holding my phone tight. Corey had collected my number to keep in touch. I still wasn't completely satisfied with him but his apology seemed heartfelt and I had to admit, he looked good to some extent.

My phone beeped and I glanced down on it. It was a text from him.

Still up?

I lifted a brow. Who knew royalty texted that simply? I was expecting to use a dictionary to reply him.

You're wondering why I text normally, aren't you?

I snorted this time.

You're right. I was expecting old English.

Common misconception. Tis the way of old to pen down as such.

I laughed out loud.

Aren't you being a bit too hypocritical?

He sent a laughing emoji.

Guilty.

I laughed again. When I was selected to go on a date with him, I was livid and refused to go until Tessa and Jay had basically kicked me out of my room and dragged me to the garden. One thing I wasn't expecting was an apology but I appreciated it either way. Maybe I was a bit too mean to him. I rolled to my side and looked at my phone. Another message entered.

Are you sleepy?

Yeah.

Alright, goodnight, Raya. Sweet dreams.

I stared at my keyboard, wondering how to reply. 'You too' seemed a bit too intimate. 'Thanks' seemed cold. I continued to stare at it before clicking on wherever came to mind and settling into my bed to sleep. I needed some time to rearrange my thoughts and feelings after that evening date.

PRINCE COREY

I waited for her message after I sent "sweet dreams". She was taking a long time to answer. Did she not like the familiarity? I hope not. Right before I was pushed to nearly delete the message, a reply came in.

Goodnight, Corey.

Simple, short and just right. I felt a smile spread on my face. I couldn't believe I was happy for just a goodnight message when I got even more detailed messages by the ladies who flirted with me.

I settled into my bed and turned off my lamp, knowing she had already gone to bed. I placed my phone on my bedside table and was just about to close my eyes when it began to vibrate. I looked at the screen to see an incoming call from an unknown person. I picked it skeptically. Not a lot of people could get my number because of who I was.

"Hello?"

"Well, hello little brother!" A lively voice chirped on the other side. "Did you miss me?"

AT THE GARDEN

"I didn't think you could play an instrument," the queen spat with venom, eyeing me as I smiled and put the violin and bow down.

"I'm talented at a lot of things," I said with a smirk. "You shouldn't underestimate me, your majesty."

She scoffed. "You're suddenly acting and talking like you intend to win."

I didn't answer and she glared at me.

"You can't be serious," she said. "You don't even want to be here."

"What I want to do or not is entirely my business, your majesty," I deflected. I wasn't ready to discuss this with her. She stomped off to the next person with a "hmph".

I looked down at my violin and sighed. What was I doing suddenly considering winning this contest? I didn't like the prince at all. Sure, he wasn't as bad as I thought but he still wasn't romantically my type. But if I were to become queen, my mother would live the life she deserved with no suffering. It was certainly something to wish for. I would try just a bit to win and if things didn't work out with him, I'd just break it off before our marriage. It sounded plausible.

"Your majesty!" A maid yelled, running towards us. The queen turned to her in surprise. "The first prince and princess are here, your majesty!"

AT THE THRONE ROOM(COREY)

My father glared at the two adults who stood in front of him, both smiling brightly. I was excited to see my older siblings after nearly five years where they left without a word. It was nice to see them again but it seemed my father didn't feel the same way.

My mother rushed into the throne room, her eyes bulging out in shock. Tears ran down her face as she stared at them. "Sara...Justin..." her voice croaked as she spoke.

My older sister and the first child smiled even brighter and walked towards my mother with her arms open. "Mother, oh, how I missed your scent." She was tall and engulfed her in a hug completely. My older brother joined them, wrapping them with his long arms. I saw my father twitch in anger at the act.

"You both have the guts to come here after your stunt five years ago?" He barked as they pulled away.

My sister scoffed. "You make it sound worse, father."

"You ran away on the day of your wedding!" He screeched before turning to his son. "And you ran with her because you were too scared to be a king!"

"Mehh," Justin shrugged. "Not scared, just not ready."

"He was a nasty eater and had sweaty palms. Ew, father," Sara scrunched her face up and crossed her arms.

I could see my father visibly rage, something he never did. He gritted his teeth in anger.

"Why did you come back?"

Sara and Justin shared a look, finally getting serious. "We realized we were a bit too childish last time. We want to apologize for that and we missed home."

Mother dabbed her tears with a handkerchief Sara gave her. "Honey, they just got back. Let's have them rest and we can talk this out later."

I looked at my father with pleading eyes. I missed my siblings far too much to watch them leave again. He took a deep breath and sighed before standing up and leaving the hall. I rushed to them and hugged them too as I had been holding myself back for father. My sister laughed heartily and hugged me tighter while my brother ruffled my hair the way he always did when I was little. I felt tears in my eyes. I missed them far too much.

7 Where it all began

RAYA

At every turn of the palace walls on my way to the garden, I could hear the mumbling of rumors of the first prince and princess. Different stories of why they left and why they came back pierced my ears. They were all wrong. I knew this because while I was passing by on my way back to my room, I had heard the royal family talking about it. I had heard almost everything and knew they'd left because of the rules of royalty. To marry someone, she didn't love. To be crowned king when he was scared. Royalty wasn't as well off as I thought, I mused.

I got to the garden to see the girls all talking. I joined Tessa and Jay and they seemed too excited to find out how the date went than to ask about the royal rumors. After the date had ended really late, I had not had the chance to see them and I spent yesterday in my room dying from cramps and talking to my mom.

"Girl, that sounds amazing!" Jay shrieked.

"At this rate, you'll be sleeping with him before I even get to talk to him," Tessa added.

"Control yourself, woman," I teased with a laugh.

A maid walked forward and clapped, drawing our attention. "Her majesty, the Queen won't be able to lead today's contest so I, head maid Yvonne, will lead it instead. Today's contest will be field work. You will be assigned to certain parts of the city to do some charity work. Whomever the people praise the most wins." She straightened up and hardened her face. "Miss Daisy Serrano.

You have been disqualified from the contests and will be sent home promptly by this afternoon."

We all turned to see the girl sobbing by the side. What could she have done?

"You ladies are henceforth not allowed to meet the prince outside the contest times where it is required. Miss Daisy had forced herself on his Highness and he has requested she be removed. No more contact with him until further notice. Is that understood?"

We nodded.

"Good. This is where you will be working," a few maids began to walk around and handed us papers with the places on them. "It begins by 12 and ends by 6. Good luck, ladies."

AT THE LOCAL FARMER'S MARKET

I lifted the crate of apples from the truck and placed it on the fruit stall.

"Thank you, young lady," the old man said, climbing out of the truck to join me.

"It's fine. I need the work out too," I said, laughing. He shut the door of the truck and entered the shop. Soon after, he came out with a small bag of fresh fruits.

"Work out all you want but make sure you stay healthy," he said with a smile. I thanked him and moved on to the next stall to help out.

I used to work part time at the local farmer's market when I was 15 and because of that, I knew most of the older people here because I had worked with them. I had been too busy to visit more often and only came by to buy things from Joe. Speaking of Joe, I needed to see him when I was done.

I walked around some more and helped more people to move things, sell things and buy things. I also helped an old couple carry their goods to their truck and the old lady had patted my cheek. It was fun to walk around here helping them and I wondered why I didn't do it more often.

A few more hours passed and it was evening, almost time to head back to the palace. I decided to go visit Joe now that I was sure I had gone to every stall.

Joe's stall stood at the entrance of the market and he sat outside, reading a magazine. I rushed forward in an attempt to scare him when I saw someone I didn't expect coming out of his stall and talking to him. It was Prince Corey.

I turned around immediately, not willing to see him after what happened this morning. Unfortunately, he had seen me and he ran towards me, calling my name.

"Raya!" He said with a smile, pulling my hand. I turned to him. He looked really pleased to see me and that made my heart flutter.

"What are you doing here?" I asked. "We're not allowed to speak with you during the contests."

"It's fine. I made sure the guards weren't around and no one else here knows you."

I narrowed my eyes at him. "You shouldn't be here."

"But I am. Here to support you and cheer you on your charity mission." He ran his hand through his dark hair. "Did you miss me?"

I felt my face heat up. My heart was racing now. Ever since we spent that evening together for the date, I had begun to feel less annoyance towards him. In fact, I was starting to enjoy our texts. "No." I quickly changed the topic. "I heard your siblings are back.

"Ah," his face widened in a childish smile. "Yes, they're back now. You have no idea how happy this makes me."

"I can guess. You look like a happy child on Christmas day. You really missed them that much huh."

We started walking towards the stall. "Yeah, but seeing you makes me even happier than I already am." He flashed a bright smile. "I missed you."

I felt my face heat up again as we entered the stall. Joe looked up from his magazine and smiled. "The lovebirds are back to where they met. I feel like Cupid for bringing you together," he said, wiping a fake tear.

I ignored him and entered inside while Corey laughed. My face was burning now and I needed a break. Now that I wasn't seeing him as an annoying prince but more like a handsome, nice man who liked me. The change was fast and made me stutter.

"Raya?" He called me from behind. "We have an hour before the contest ends. Wanna hang out in here?"

I stared at him, rethinking my decision to choose to be in the contests and be with him. It was tricky but I was starting to like him a bit more than I intended.

"Yes," I said, deciding to take the leap and trust my guts. "I'd love to hang out with you."

8 disqualified

PRINCE COREY

I make my way towards the garden entrance to watch the girls. After the evening I spent with Raya, I realized that she was much softer and sweeter than I ever imagined. She didn't bite back when I sat close to her and whenever I expressed myself and how I felt for her, I saw a small blush that made my heart skip. I was calling for her already and it was an amazing feeling.

I heard a commotion as I neared the garden. It sounded like two people shouting. I rushed forward and stopped at the entrance of the garden to see Jessica and Raya arguing and my mother in the back frowning in disapproval.

I walked towards them. "What in the world is going on here?"

My mother looked at me and sighed.

"Raya broke the rules and was with the prince during a contest yesterday!" Jessica yelled with a devilish smile on her face and grabbed Raya's hand. The rest of the girls stared on in silence and shock, wondering why she would do that.

"That's not exactly what happened," Raya said, yanking her hand out if Jessica's grip.

"Yeah, yeah," Jessica mocked. "You want to say again that it was a coincident that you met together at your charity spot and spent time with each other? Or about how you didn't want to but the prince offered to hang out?" She scoffed.

"I'm saying the truth!" I yelled out.

"Why would the prince want to hang out with someone like you when you insult him and disrespect him?" The queen asked harshly.

"Because he likes..." She trailed off, covering her mouth with her hand.

The girls gasped and Tessa and Jay looked at each other.

"What?" The queen finally said. "The prince likes you?"

"Wait, I didn't-" I began to say.

"You dare say lies against the prince so blatantly?" She barked. Raya took a step back when she stepped forward. "You? The same person who disrespected him and tried to fail intentionally? You?"

"Mother!" I called, stepping in between the both of them. My mother glared at me. "She's not lying. I did see her there coincidentally."

"She tricked you, son."

"No, I tricked her. I saw her there and approached her myself. I offered for us to hang out even when she refused. It was all me!"

My mother glared at me even harder. "Now she makes you lie?"

"No, she doesn't. I'm telling the truth."

"Guards!" She called, stepping back. "Take this woman and escort her out." She turned to Raya. "You are hereby disqualified from the contest. I don't ever want to see you near my son again."

Raya looked crestfallen as the guards approached her. One of the laid their hand on her shoulder and she shrugged him off.

"Don't touch her!" I yelled. My mother gasped, seeing me react like that for Raya. She had no idea how much I wanted to be with her.

"I can walk by myself," Raya spat, stomping out of the garden. I watched her walk away with pain in my heart. I didn't want her to leave. I clenched my fists in anger and turned to glare at Jessica. She yelped and stepped back, colliding into some girls behind her. I turned to my mother next and she glared back at me. I stormed off, anger brewing in me. I needed to stop Raya from leaving.

RAYA

The guards waiting outside my room were a clear reminder of what had just happened. I stuffed my things into my bag, feeling less angry and more despaired. I was finally starting to like someone but now, we're being ripped apart because of a stupid jealous girl. It annoyed me to think about but there was nothing I could do to change it.

I grabbed my bags and stepped out, heading out of the palace. On the corridor, I heard Tessa and Jay yelling out my name and running to me. One of the guards made to stop them but Tessa kicked him in the groin, making him fall. The others took a step back from her and Jay hugged me.

"What are you guys doing here?" I asked. Tessa hugged me too.

"We had to see you before you went," Jay said.

"Yeah, we know you weren't lying."

"But the contests...you could be disqualified for talking to me." I reminded them.

"Well, it doesn't matter. Sis before dicks," Tessa giggled. "I'd pick you over a prince any day."

"Me too," Jay said. I hugged them again, tightening my arms around them.

"I'll see you both outside, I guess."

"Yup. Don't go ahead and lose your virginity before I get back. I want to hear the details of your dates with the prince too, you sneaky rat," Tessa grinned, earning a slap on the back from Jay.

"Take care of yourself, Raya," Jay said.

"You too."

They left and the guards escorted me to my home to meet my mom. She hugged me tight and asked if I was fine. I nodded and smiled at her before heading to my room. The moment I dropped my bag on the floor and touched my bed, the tears began to flow. I never thought I'd cry over a guy and he wasn't the only reason I was crying. The humiliation. The lies. The chance to make my mom happy. And him. It all tore me down to tears and I sat still on my bed, letting it all flow.

What a happy birthday to me.

9 I'm Leaving

PRINCE COREY

A month had passed since Raya was disqualified after what happened. I had search everywhere to find her but couldn't find her to this day. I had asked my trusted bodyguard B to help me out but my mother had banned him from helping me in any matter involving. Even our private instigators and everyone who possibly find her were banned from helping me. Her phone number had somehow disappeared from my phone and I was stranded, unable to see her again.

I sat at the garden on the same spot we had our date and stared into the orange sky. The sun was setting just like it did on our date. I sighed and closed my eyes, breathing in the fresh air. A hand is placed on my shoulder and I open my eyes to see someone standing above me with a smile on her mouth.

"Sherry."

"Your Highness," she cooed with her soft voice. She had won the contest after Jessica was disqualified for cheating in the charity event by trying to pay the people off instead of working. Sherry wasn't a horrible person but she wasn't good either. She got angry at the maids easily and never did anything by herself because she knew the maids would clean up and my mother would support her. I disliked it.

"What are you doing out here?" I asked. She normally never left her large room.

"The sunset looks beautiful from here," she replied, sitting beside me. "I had to see it."

She leaned on me, resting her head on my shoulder but I jerked her off and stood. She glared at me.

"You can't keep pushing me away, Corey," she said angrily. "I'm your fiancée. Stop thinking about that girl."

"I can't stop," I muttered. "Every day and every night, I think about her. I know it's not your fault and you don't deserve to deal with my emotions but I can't just push her out of my mind."

Sherry stood up angrily. "What does she have that I don't?"

I didn't answer. It wasn't something I could speak of.

She glared at me before storming off, cursing. I sighed and sat back on the chair. Sherry didn't deserve this. She deserved someone who cared about her and didn't think about someone else when she was right there. I could feel the guilt eating me up but I couldn't help it. I was already in love with someone else. I just wished I could meet her someway, somehow.

RAYA

"I'm coming!" I yelled, running to the door. Someone had been knocking over and over again and it was getting frustrating. I yanked the door open. "My mother isn't home so if there's a message I can..." My jaw nearly dropped.

Standing in front of me in their sheer glory, the stunning older siblings of the prince stood, a snug smile on their faces.

"I told you I'd find her in two hours," the princess said, letting herself in.

"Yeah, yeah. Just your luck," the first prince countered as he followed her in.

I stared at them in utter disbelief. The famous older children of the king and queen stood in my home. It was even more surprising than living in the palace for a week because they were known for being unbelievably perfect. Now, I saw why. They looked like a god and a goddess blessing me with their presence.

"Raya?" Sara called, snapping me out of my reverie.

"Your Highness!" I said louder than I intended. "It's an honor to have you both in my home. What brings you here?"

Justin laughed. "I heard she was rude and arrogant."

Sara joined him. "I guess it's only to the wrong people."

It seemed like they'd heard about my antics in the palace. I felt my face redden in embarrassment.

They sat on the couch and I sat in front of them. "Is there anything you'd like to drink?" I offered. Tessa and Jay would die if they heard what was happening right now.

"No thanks. We're only gonna be here for a while," Sara answered curtly.

I nodded and sat upright.

"Our brother," she started. "You like him, don't you?"

The room went silent enough that I could hear my own breathing. "Your Highness..." I said after a while. "His Highness, Prince Corey is engaged to be married in two days."

"So?" Justin laughed. "Sara ran away on her freaking wedding day."

"You should have seen me running in my red dress. I looked stunning." They laughed again.

I noticed how much they laughed with each other and felt myself relax.

"Well?" Justin asked. "Do you like him?"

I stared at my hands in silence. "It doesn't matter."

"It does," he said. "Until he says 'I do', it still matters."

I looked up, feeling fear in my heart. "But the queen-"

"The queen wants her son to be happy," Sara interjected. "And being with that...girl doesn't make him happy. It makes him miserable. She doesn't like that."

I frowned. "Then why was she so against us being together?"

Justin burst into laughter and Sara slapped his back. The reminded me so much of Tessa and Jay.

"Well, you did disrespect them both in front of others MULTIPLE TIMES and said you were going to fail intentionally so of course she didn't trust you with her son."

I mulled it over. She was right. I had ruined the first impression she had of me and she was just trying to protect her son. "Ah. I fucked up."

"Indeed, you did. Now you have to fix it."

I looked up to see them standing. "But I'm not allowed in the palace."

"Scale the fence."

"It's not that easy, your Highness."

"Ughhhhhhhh," Sara moaned. "You're boring. If you're not ready to fight for him, then don't."

I sighed. I needed to say it. "I'm leaving the kingdom."

They froze.

"I got a scholarship to study Fashion Designing in another kingdom. I leave in two days."

They both stared at me in surprise.

"Uh, congratulations," Justin said.

"Thank you," I sniffed. "I can't abandon my dreams and ambitions for him. I'm sorry." I could feel the tears rising in my eyes. I was being a crybaby.

"Hush, it's fine," Sara said, hugging me. "I understand too. Truth be told, I didn't really hate my ex-boyfriend. I wanted to see the world but marrying him meant stopping myself. I totally understand." She wiped the tear that fell to my cheek. "Never stop your dreams for anyone. I'm sure he'll understand."

I sniffed again and nodded. They left not long after, leaving me to my thoughts. I went upstairs to my room and dropped to my bed with a heavy feeling in my chest. I didn't want to leave like this. It was too much. But I couldn't stay either because this was a big opportunity for me. I would go and make a name for myself and find someone to love and make my mother happy. That's all that matters. I buried my face into my pillow and screamed. There was no doubting the fact that I was tired. Emotionally and physically.

10 I object

RAYA

I pulled my suitcase out of the house and into the porch. It was really cold out so I had on a parka and a scarf. My mother was already waiting for me at the airport with rest of my luggage while I stayed back to say goodbye to my friends and lock up the house. It had taken longer than I planned because Tessa started crying until Jay started crying too and I started crying and it became a sob fest. After I managed to peel away from them, I went home to get my dad's pendant that I had forgotten on my bed. I couldn't go anywhere without it.

Tessa and Jay had wanted to come drop me at the airport but I refused. If I saw them again, I'd cry all the way into the plane. I couldn't handle that.

I stood at the porch and stared at the house I had spent 18 years in. From the memories from when I was younger to the last two months with the whole prince drama to this moment right here.

I sighed. "I'll miss you, big old home," I said, patting the porch railing.

I pulled my suitcase down and began to roll it away from my home and towards my future.

PRINCE COREY

The priest's words barely landed on my ear with the loud noise of my racing heart. It was my wedding day and I could not feel the slightest emotion for the woman standing in front of me and smiling. She looked beautiful but she wasn't the face I wanted to see on the altar. If was someone else. Someone I could find no matter how I searched.

"...speak now or forever hold your peace."

The hall was silent.

Deep down, I prayed for one person to say something, anything against the marriage even if just to give me time to breathe. I looked to my mother. She stared at me with tears in her eyes. Whether of joy or sorrow, I had no idea. She wasn't going to speak either way. My father sat beside her and refused to speak either. It was simple, really.

They made the rules for the contest. They couldn't just back up now. I couldn't back up either because I had chosen this on my own. A royal should never go back on his word.

"Now, you may say your-"

"I object!" A loud voice yelled as the double doors were banged open. My older siblings stood at the door, smiling widely.

"Fuck, I've always wanted to do that," Sara laughed as she stomped towards us. She climbed onto the altar and cleared her throat. "This man," she said as she pointed at me, "does not love this woman," she pointed at Sherry. "And this woman does not love this man. They shouldn't be together. End of story."

I stood there in shock. I had prayed to be removed from this marriage but not like this. "What are you-"

"My little brother, Prince Corey is in love with someone else. She's not here. In fact, she's on her way out of the kingdom because she can't stand the fact, he's marrying someone else." The church had a collective gasp. "And this woman is in love with that man over there," she said, pointing to a young man crying on one of the chairs. "They've been dating but she was forced to be with the prince by her stepmother." When the gasps came again, she laughed. "Iconic, I know."

"Sara!" Our father stood, gripping the arm of his chair tightly. "What in heaven's name do you think you're doing?"

"Doing what you failed to do for me as a father five years ago. Saving him from the sad life grandfather and grandmother lived in because of this stupid tradition. Not everyone is lucky enough to find love like you and mom did!"

Father was raging. "You better get down here this instant-"

"I object too," my mother said quietly. She wiped the tears in her eyes. "I just wanted you to be happy. But this.... this doesn't make you happy, does it?"

I shook my head and she nodded. "Let's cancel the wedding. Let the children have what they want."

The church was quiet for a while until Sherry screeched and ran to the man in the chair.

"Kennedy!" She yelled, smashing his face in a kiss. Jessica who sat at a corner saw this and fainted into her mother's arms.

I looked at her and smiled. I'd never seen her so happy. But there was something off. "Wait. What did you say about Raya leaving?"

"Ah," Justin said. He pulled out an envelope and handed it to me. "She's on her way to Rowland Kingdom."

"Rowland?" Mother asked. "That's 13 hours away."

"Yup, which is why you need to go see her now, Corey," Sara said. "Before she leaves."

"The kingdom," father said with a tired look. "What about the royal family? Who will be king?"

Justin smirked. "I'll be king. On one condition."

Father frowned. "What is it?"

"Abolish the marriage tradition. It's caused more harm than good."

Father stared at him for a few minutes before giving in. "Fine."

"Also!" Sara added. "Princesses can choose who they marry."

"You said one condition."

"Take it or leave it, your majesty."

He sighed. "Fine. You were too good for that boy anyway."

"Yes!" Sara and Justin high fived. I stood there, standing with the envelope in my hands.

"Well, don't just stand there," mother said with a smile. "Go get your bride."

I looked at all of them. My family. "Thank you," I whispered before racing out of the church.

"Your Highness!" I heard a voice yell. It was B in a car. "Need a ride?"

RAYA

I sat waiting for my turn to get on the plane. My mother had left to check my bags one last time while I waited. I was finally about to leave and explore my dream. I could feel a lump in my throat while I sat. It was scary.

The announcement for my plane rang out and I stood up. I would wait at the entrance to the loading bridge.

Immediately I stood up, I heard a sound behind me. I turned back to see someone I never thought I'd see any time soon.

"Raya!" He yelled, running towards me.

"Corey?"

He engulfed me in a tight hug while he panted. He must have rushed all the way from the palace. His scent filled my nose and felt tears in my eyes again.

"Corey, what are you doing here?" I asked when he finally let me go.

"I couldn't let you leave like this, I..." He trailed off, staring at me. "I love you."

My face heated up faster than I could keep up. "But your wedding-"

"Cancelled. I can't marry anyone else except you, Raya. Please believe me."

I believed him. But I was about to leave. I heard the announcer call my plane number. "I have to leave."

"Wait!" He called, holding my hands. "I promise to come see you there as soon as I can so, please," he squeezed my hand. "Wait for me."

I could feel myself choking up. Instead of trying to speak, I nodded. There were no words for this moment. In one single swoop, his lips fell on mine, devouring me in a breathtaking kiss. I've had kisses before but nothing like this. I tightened my arms around his neck and leaned into him. It felt amazing.

"Get a room!" Someone called and people laughed. We broke apart, giggling like little children.

"I love you," he whispered, placing us forehead against mine.

"I love you too," I said to him, hugging him again.

I felt a crinkle of paper underneath me and looked down. It was an envelope. Corey watched as I picked it up.

"Sara and Justin gave it to me. I don't know why though."

I opened the envelope to see two plane tickets for first class assigned to both of us. I couldn't help but chuckle as I pulled them out.

"Corey," I said.

"Yes?"

"Would you like to be with me in Rowland?"

I heard his breath hitch before he muttered a yes and repeated again loudly.

I hugged him tight, kissing him again and holding the tickets carefully in my hand.

It would take us to where we would be together, undisturbed by the royal rules or anything. Where we could be us. Just little children in love with each other.

THREE YEARS LATER

RAYA

I glanced at the picture frame sitting on my bedside table and smiled. It was an early autumn morning so I got up from the bed, took a bath and made my way downstairs for a cup of coffee. The blinds on the kitchen window were lifted so I got a good look at the woods in the backyard. I wondered where he had gone so early since he was neither inside nor in the backyard.

I decided to get ready for school and just call him when I get there. I grabbed my coat and keys then ran out into the streets littered with fallen leaves. My ride was already waiting for me by the roadside and I chuckled as I got into the car.

"You're late," he said. I dumped my bag into the backseat and strapped the seatbelt across me.

"You should try calling me when you get here. I'm not superhuman, you know," I replied. Tyler rolled his eyes and turned on the engine before driving out into the road. I was so stressed out about my final exam I was constantly sick in the stomach.

"Tyler, pull over please hurry," I said to him. I could feel it about to come up. Once Tyler pulled the car over, I quickly opened the door and began to vomit.

"Jesus Raya, are you pregnant? I haven't seen that much vomit since Jay was pregnant with Raymond." Tyler implied to me. Pregnancy has never once crossed my mind. I know I was just stressed from all these finals. I then closed the car door.

"Do you have a napkin or something up there?" I asked him as I was out of breath from vomiting. He then reached in the glove compartment and reached back by handing me a napkin. I then began to wipe around my mouth.

"And to answer your question, I have been stressing out over these past couple of weeks about the finals. The thought of knowing now will either be the end or the beginning of my career was driving me fucking crazy," I informed Tyler.

"If you say so Raya." Tyler implied and I couldn't help but to check my calendar. Shit. I was late.

The rest of the trip was silent with me going through flash cards for my final paper and my thoughts of being late. Not only was exam week a horror to experience but now I'm about to stress out about this.

"Working on your final paper?" He asked, making a turn down the road.

"Mmhmm," I muttered, flipping to the next card.

"Isn't your department done with exams?" He asked me curiously.

"Yeah, it's an extra course. I need the boost in my G.P.A" I implied.

He groaned. "I wish I could do that too. My courses are already too difficult to deal with. I can't even consider extras."

I laughed. "I didn't tell you to go for a medical course."

"But you didn't stop me either." He said to me sarcastically.

"Touché." I giggled.

We got to the school gates a few minutes later and I got out the car. "Where are you going from here?" I asked, pulling out my bag from the backseat.

"Gotta go pick up our kid." He explained.

I snorted. "Jay would kill me if she found out I was stealing her husband AND her kid."

Tyler laughed. We said our goodbyes and I headed to class to join the rest of my course mates do some last-minute studying, I decided to send Tessa a message. I needed to see her.

While I was reading to myself, I suddenly went blind. Someone had covered my eyes with their hands. I stayed quiet for a while, thinking about the texture of the hand and who it was. With a smile, I called out their name and they puffed in annoyance.

"You always get me," Tessa said, taking her hands off my face and sitting beside me.

"You do this every day." I reminded her.

"Tsk," she muttered, flipping through her books. "Are you ready for the exam? I also brought what you asked for."

I sighed and looked at my book. "Not exactly."

"Didn't you study last night? You have eye bags." She asked.

I gave her a wild smile. "I did stay up all night, but not to study." I winked.

She tilted her head, frowning. "Then what kept you up like...oh. You little rat. Maybe that's why you're in this situation now."

I giggled and focused on my books again. "He's been busy with royal affairs lately so we don't do it as much as we used to. I didn't have the heart to tell him I had an exam today."

"Doesn't he ALWAYS ask you for your timetable?" Tessa asked.

"Yeah, but he probably forgot. He's so cute." I answered.

Tessa rolled her eyes. "You and Jay act the same name. Damn couples."

We studied a little more until it was time for the exam. Tessa and I sat separately because of our class numbers. The exam wasn't too difficult but I was expecting a B or a C+, not an A. In an hour and a half, it finally ended and Tessa and I left the hall together, talking as we headed to the bathroom.

"You got it didn't you?" I asked her as we walked inside the bathroom.

"You bet your ass I did." She informed me as she reached in her purse and handed me the pregnancy test.

I began to sigh.

"Are you nervous?" She asked curiously.

"I nervous as fuck. But we're here now so let's do it." I told her as she nodded and I headed into the bathroom stall. Once I got into the bathroom stall, I opened the box and pulled out the directions before I took the test. As I finished up, I sat the test down and began to wash my hands. My nerves were a wreck. I wanted too through up all over again.

As moments went by, we just stood there in silence. I had refused to look.

"You want me to look?" Tessa asked me and I nodded. Tessa then walked over to the test and picked it up and looked at me.

"Well congratulations. You are official holding another Aire to the throne." She informed me and she began to get excited.

"You're kidding me." I yelled out as I snatched the test from her to look at the results myself. I was indeed pregnant. I was so caught up in getting myself together for this test I didn't even realize that I was already two weeks late.

"I'm shocked. I honestly don't know what to say." I whispered out and Tessa began to hug me.

"I can't believe my best friend is having a baby by a Prince!" She yelled out in excitement. I began to smile. I couldn't believe it myself. Sometimes I still can't believe that he even chose me.

"Let's get out of here," Tessa stated as she then wrapped her arm around my neck and we headed out the bathroom. She was overly excited.

"Have you seen Jay lately? I can't wait until she finds out" Tessa said.

"I haven't seen her in a few days now." I responded. "Tyler said she's hibernating. She's having a period so he's taking care of little Ray for now."

"Still can't believe she named her kid after you."

"Me neither."

"I wanted to do it first."

I blushed. "Why?"

"BECAUSE," she exaggerated, "you have odd good luck. That's what Jay said when she named Raymond."

I stuffed my hands into my pocket, smiling sheepishly.

"I'm honored," I said.

Tessa was quiet for a while. "I know someone else who's about to be honored," she said slyly before pointing ahead.

I followed her hand and my eyes landed on Corey. I handed my bag to Tessa and began to run into his open arms, seeing his eyes sparkle when I jumped into his arms. I tightened my hold on him just as he did to me and he twirled me around.

"Corey," I gushed, nuzzling his chest. "I missed you."

He chuckled and I felt his chest vibrate under me. I loved the sound of it. "I missed you too, Ray."

We finally pulled away from each other only for him to kiss me frantically, holding my face between his large hands. I giggled and pulled away again.

I finally looked at him and noticed something different. "You're all dressed up. Are you just coming back from a meeting?" I mused, eyeing his black suit. Some girls stared as they walked by but I wasn't worried. He was mine and mine alone.

"Uh, yeah," he answered and held my hand tightly. "I have a surprise for you." He began to pull me forward. I turned back to see Tessa but she just waved at me with a grin. What's going on?

We got into his car and drove for almost an hour. I kept asking where we were going but he never responded to it. He looked nervous and I was starting to get worried. We finally got to a wide clearing of grass at the edge of town. It was quiet, the only sounds being the chirping of birds and the soft whispered of the wind against the grass. I stepped out of the car, walking towards the one thing that caught my attention.

The beautiful sunset against an orange sky.

I smiled as I stared at it. "This is beautiful, Core," I said, dipping my hands in my pocket. I was nervous. How was he going to react to the news I about the baby?

"Yeah," he said and stood behind me, wrapping his arms around me. "I came across this place a week ago and all I could think of was you."

I blushed and turned to kiss his cheek. "It reminds me of our first date in the palace. Except it's lacking the dislike and the cupcakes."

He chuckled. We were both silent as we watched the sun descend into the sea beneath it. After a few minutes, he spoke again. "Time sure flies, huh."

I leaned against him. "Yeah. It's been three years since then. We've grown so much."

"And I still love you, Raya, and I'll love you right to my grave and to the afterlife." He pulled away and I stood still, worry clouding my mind. He was being odd. Was he going away? Did his family want him to come back? Was he leaving? Worry turned to fear while the thoughts raced in my head.

"Raya?" He called from behind. I turned to him slowly, afraid to hear what he might say. What I saw instead wasn't what I expected.

He was kneeling on one knee, holding a ring box in his right hand and holding it open with his left. "And I want to spend the rest of my life loving you. So, would you let me?"

I felt my world spin and my breath hitch. My hands trembled at my side as I watched him kneeling before, *proposing* to me.

"Core..." I muttered. I couldn't believe it.

"Raya, I want to be with you for the rest of my life," he said. "Will you marry me?"

I nodded erratically, tears running down my face. "Yes," I stuttered, crying even more when he took my hand and slid the ring into my finger. He got up and wrapped me in a hug before kissing my cheeks where my tears poured.

"I have something to tell you" I informed him.

"Everything ok?" He asked me as he began to hold me close. I breathed out heavily and let out a sigh.

"I'm pregnant Core…. We're pregnant." I told him and he pulled me into a passionate kiss.

"I love you, Raya St. Thomas. Forever. This is forever."
"I love you too. Forever and After."

The End

ABOUT THE AUTHOR

Currently a native from Goose Creek, South Carolina, Michelle is a mother of two beautiful children. Since she was a child, she always loved reading books. As she got older her love for reading never once died. She spent so much money on paying to read other stories she came up with the idea to write a book on her own. She loves to read romance drama books. So, her dedication to read these books eventually became her passion to write them. She is currently studying in book publishing and is starting her dream to open up her own book publishing company. She believes everyone's success starts with a form of reading.

Don't miss out!

Visit the website below and you can sign up to receive emails whenever Michelle Robinson publishes a new book. There's no charge and no obligation.

https://books2read.com/r/B-A-NJTY-RMWJC

BOOKS 2 READ

Connecting independent readers to independent writers.

Also by Michelle Robinson

If Only You Knew
If Only You Knew

Standalone
Twisted: A Cinderella Story
The Billionaires Touch